For Mark, with my love xx – T C

To the lovely Gu – G S

First published in the United States in 2014
Capstone Young Readers, a Capstone Imprint
1710 Roe Crest Dr., North Mankato, MN 56003
www.capstoneyoungreaders.com

First published in Great Britain in 2011 by Little Tiger Press under the title Little Penguin Lost

Text copyright © Tracey Corderoy 2011 • Illustrations copyright © Gavin Scott 2011
Tracey Corderoy and Gavin Scott have asserted their rights to be identified
as the author and illustrator of this work under the Copyright,
Designs and Patents Act, 1988

Library of Congress Cataloging-in-Publication data is availble on the Library of Congress website
ISBN 978-1-62370-116-1 (hardcover) ISBN 978-1-62370-117-8 (paperback)

LTP/1800/0790/1013

Lost Little PENGUIN

by Tracey Corderoy · illustrated by Gavin Scott

capstone
young readers

Three little roly-poly penguins were having their afternoon snack. Percy and Posy were eating up nicely. But Plip was too busy playing with his favorite toy.

"Hey, Plip," said Percy. "Finish your fish or Wal-the-Wump will snap it up."

"Who's scared of a grumpy old walrus?" giggled Plip. "Not me!"

After their snack, it was time to swim.
But Plip had to keep his toy dry.
  "Oh, Plip!" sighed Posy. "Swim like
us or one day Wal-the-Wump might
catch you."
  "Wal-the-Wump?" giggled Plip.
"He doesn't scare me!"

When the penguins were too shivery to swim anymore, they played Wal-the-Wump games instead.

"Raggh!" growled Posy.

"I'm Wal. And I'm coming to get you!"

"My turn!" cried Plip, wobbling uphill
and trying to look big and scary.
"I'm Wal-the-Wump and I'll squash
you flat! Hee hee!"

They played together all afternoon.

Then, suddenly, Plip went quiet.

"Hungry?" asked Posy.

"Sleepy?" Percy said.

But Plip just opened his beak
and wailed . . .

"WHERE'S MY SOCKYBUG?"

Everyone searched for
Plip's little sock toy.
    They checked under
the water . . .

then inside all
the caves.

"Where can he be?" sighed Plip.
"He'll be wanting a cuddle soon."

They were still searching when big snow clouds
gathered and the sky grew dark and stormy.

Percy put a wing around Plip's shoulder.

"You're a big boy now," he said. "You don't
need a baby toy, do you?"

"But he's not a toy," sniffed Plip.
"He's my friend."

They were just about to head back
home when: "Wait!" cried Plip.
"I think I know where I left him!"
He shot away over the hill as
snow began to fall.
"Sockybug!" he called . . .

"I'm coming to get you!"

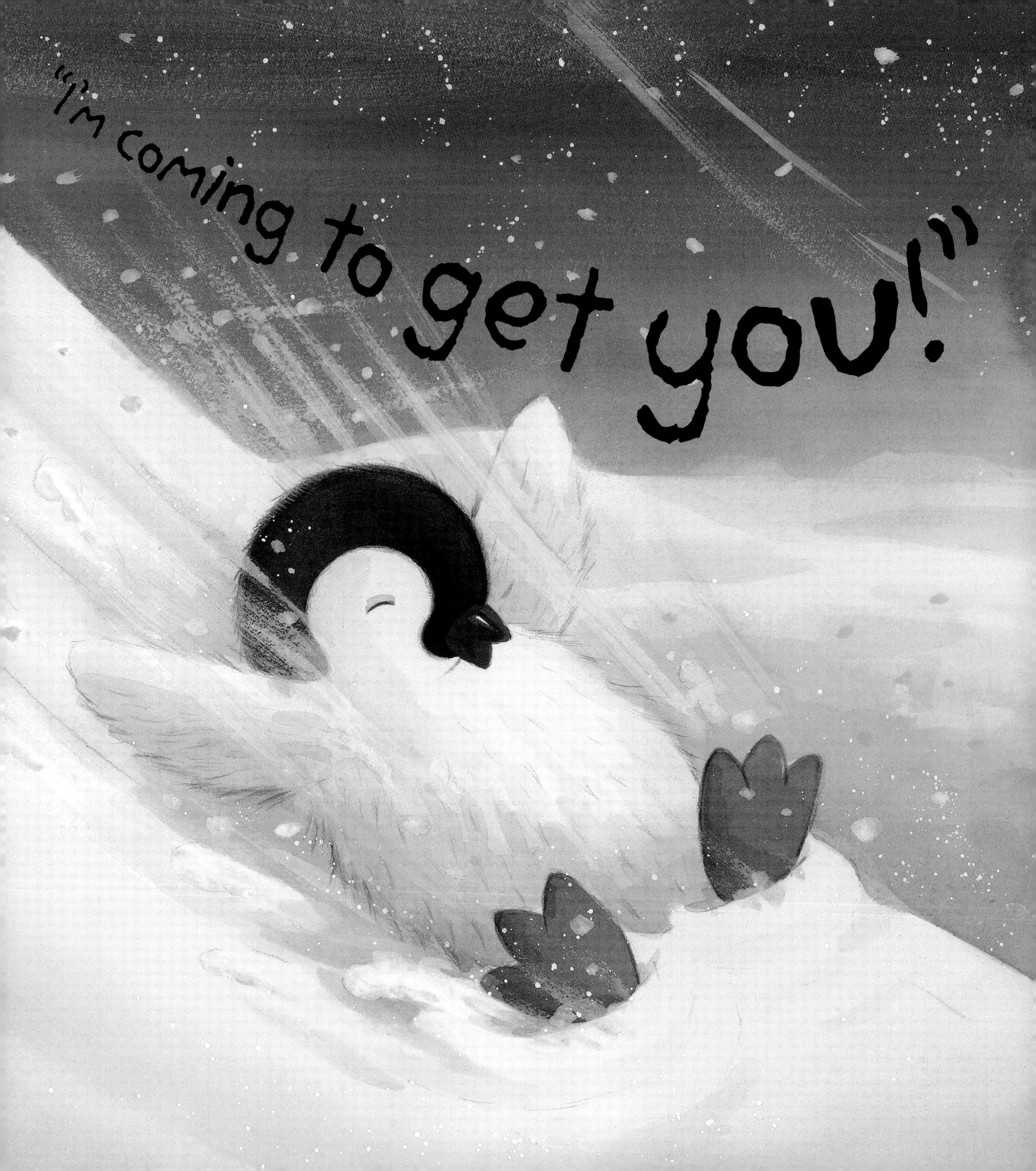

Percy and Posy raced after Plip
through the tumbling snow.
"Come back!" they yelled.
Then, suddenly, Percy gave a
great gasp, "Oh no!"

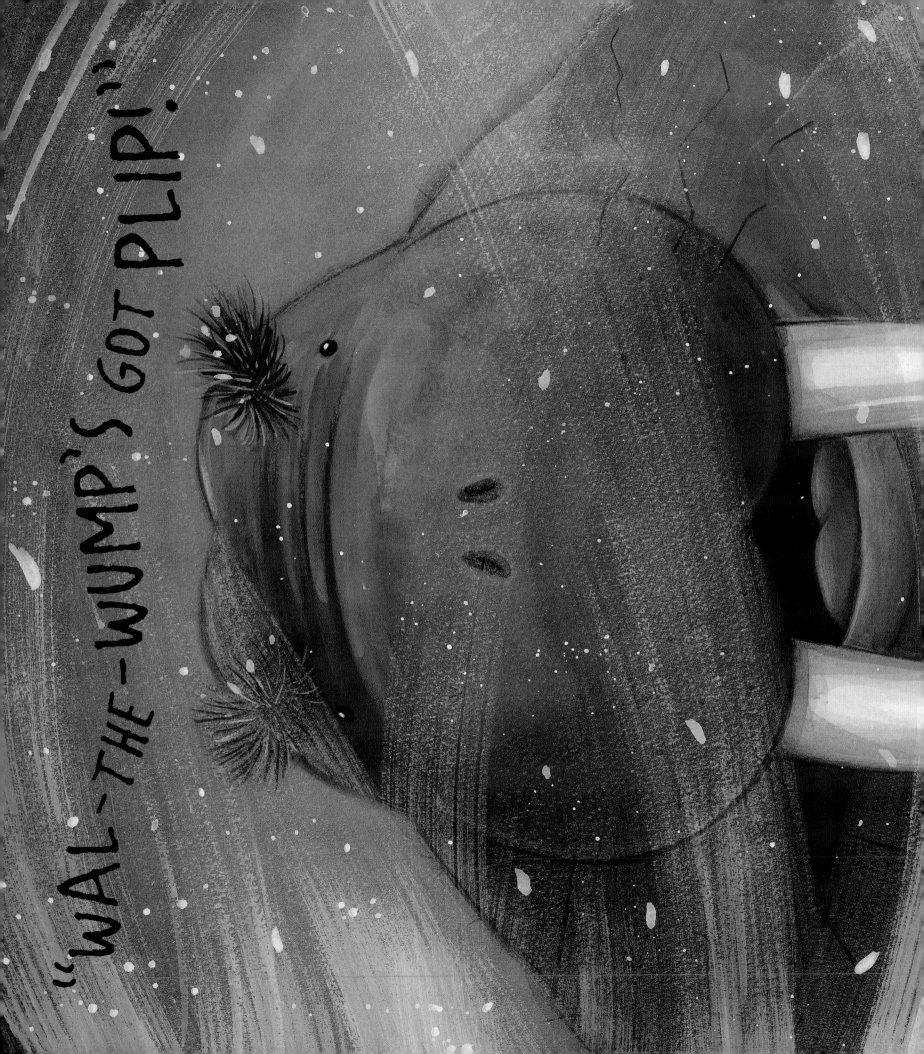

"WAL-THE-WUMP'S GOT PLIP!"

The walrus's enormous teeth
flashed as his jaws opened wide . . . .

And Wal let out a gigantic guffaw.
"Tickle, tickle!" chuckled Plip.
Then he turned to his brother and
sister. "Wal found my Sockybug! Look!" he cried.

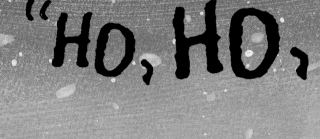

"HO, HO,

HO!"

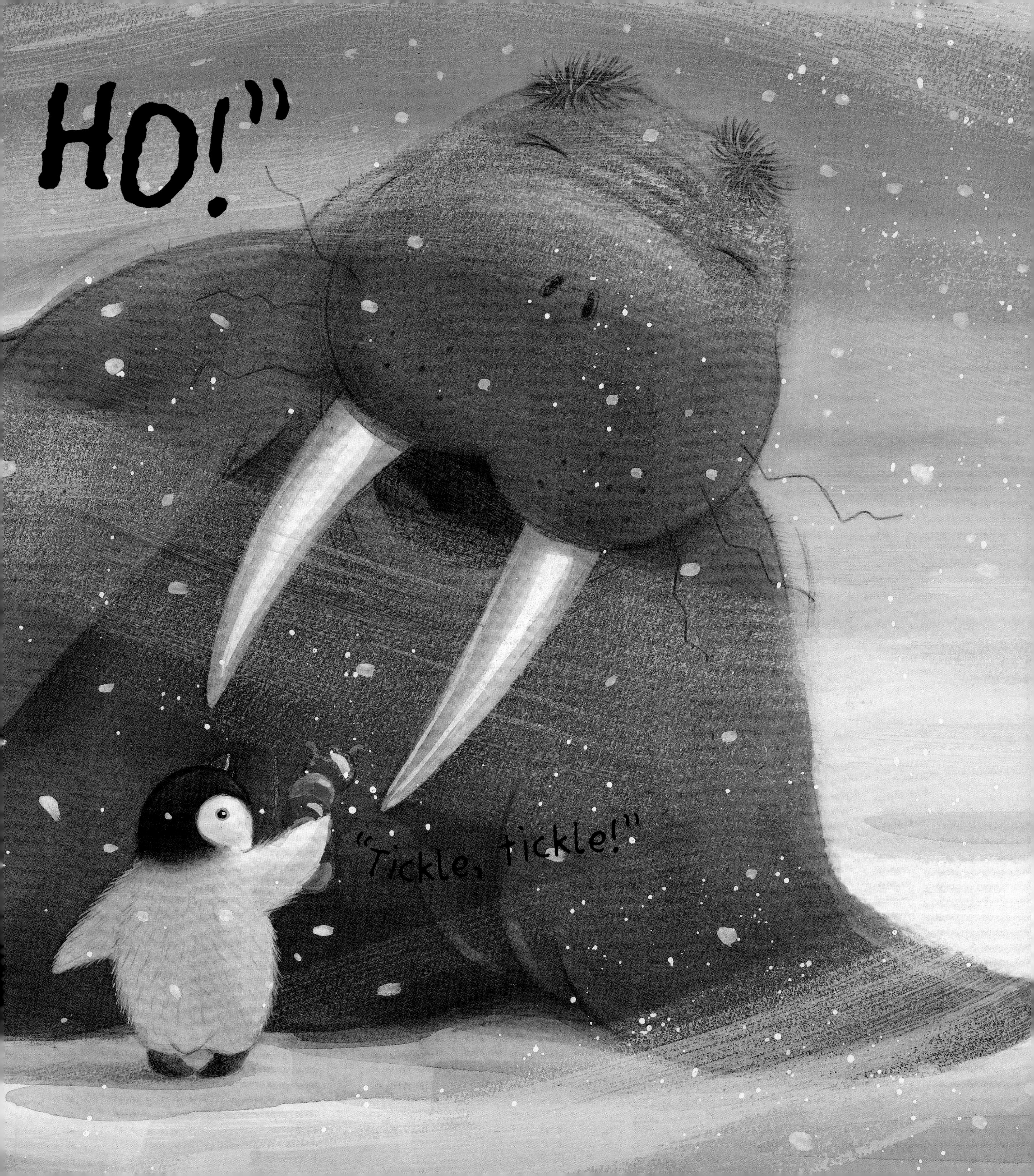

"Tickle, tickle!"

After that, Plip made everyone
their very own Sockybugs.
And from then on, tickle time
was the best time of the day!